W9-CKP-947

MO
to the Rescue

MO
to the Rescue

MARY POPE OSBORNE

PICTURES BY

DyAnne DiSalvo-Ryan

DIAL BOOKS FOR YOUNG READERS
NEW YORK

For Shy Dog Lemon-Pope
M.P.O.

To Ed and John
D.D.

Published by Dial Books for Young Readers
A Division of NAL Penguin Inc.
2 Park Avenue
New York, New York 10016

Published simultaneously in Canada by
Fitzhenry & Whiteside Limited, Toronto

Text copyright © 1985 by Mary Pope Osborne
Pictures copyright © 1985 by DyAnne DiSalvo-Ryan
All rights reserved.
Printed in Hong Kong by South China Printing Co.
The Dial Easy-to-Read logo is a registered trademark of
Dial Books for Young Readers,
a division of NAL Penguin Inc., ® TM 1,162,718.

Library of Congress Cataloging in Publication Data
Osborne, Mary Pope. Mo to the rescue.
Summary: Mo, a good-natured sheriff, does his best to protect
the members of his rural community, who are also his friends.
1. Children's stories, American. [1. Sheriffs—Fiction.
2. Friendship—fiction. 3. Animals—Fiction.]
I. DiSalvo-Ryan, DyAnne, ill. II. Title.
PZ7.081167Mo 1985 [E] 84-28796
COBE

First Hardcover Printing 1985
ISBN 0-8037-0180-2 (tr.)
ISBN 0-8037-0182-9 (lib.bdg.)
1 3 5 7 9 10 8 6 4 2

First Trade Paperback Printing 1987
ISBN 0-8037-0440-2 (ppr.)
1 3 5 7 9 10 8 6 4 2

The full-color artwork was prepared using pencil, colored pencil,
and watercolor washes. It was then color-separated and
reproduced as red, blue, yellow, and black halftones.

Reading Level 2.1

Contents

SHERIFF MO

One day Mo took a walk along
the bank of Smith Pond.
Mockingbirds sang
and cattails blew in the breeze.

"Hi, Sheriff. How's it going?"
asked Peewee the rat.

"Fine," said Mo.

"You look nice today, Sheriff,"
said Peewee's girlfriend, Pearl.

"Thank you, Pearl," said Mo.

Mo walked down to the pond
and took off his shoes and socks.
"Ah, that feels good," he said
as he wiggled his toes.

Then he waded into the water.
"What a day, what a day," he said.
"I think it stinks," said a voice.

"Goodness," said Mo. "Who said that?"

"Chicken Lucille," said the voice.

Mo looked behind a bush.

A chicken was sitting

on her suitcase in the shade.

She was wearing

baggy bermuda shorts

and large tennis shoes.

"Hello," said Mo.

"Are you new to this area?"

"Yes, I'm sorry to say,"

said Chicken Lucille.

"You don't like it here?" said Mo.

11

"I certainly don't!" she said.

"Why not?" asked Mo.

"No friends!" she cried.

"Goodness," said Mo.

"We can't have that.

Come with me, Lucille."

The chicken picked up her suitcase and walked with Mo.

"Meet my friend Lucille,"
Mo said to Pearl and Peewee.

"Oh, I like your shorts, Lucille,"
said Pearl.

"Well, thank you, honey," said Lucille.

"Have you guys met Lucille?"
Mo asked the Bluejay family.

"Hey, meet my friend Lucille!"
he shouted to the frogs and water fleas.
"This is Chicken Lucille,
a new friend of mine,"
he told the ducks and loons.

At the end of the day
Mo took Lucille to
Aunt Minnie's boardinghouse
and said good-bye to her.

"You're very sweet, Sheriff,"
Lucille said.

Mo's face got red.

"Oh—just doing my job, Lucille,"
he said.

THE FIGHT

One bright morning
Mo was hanging his clothes
in the sun to dry.
Suddenly Pearl ran by.

"Help, Sheriff!" she yelled.

"A fight!"

"Oh, no," said Mo.

"Let's hurry!"

Mo followed Pearl into the woods.

Loud squawks and squeaks

were coming from the top of a tree.

"It's the Bluejays," Peewee said.
"They're fighting again!"
"Goodness," said Mo.
Leaves and twigs were flying
through the air.

"Stop those birds, Sheriff!"

Pearl cried.

"Indeed, I will," Mo said.

"Bring me a stepladder

and a bedspread."

The animals looked at one another.

"A stepladder?" said Aunt Minnie.

"A bedspread?" said Chicken Lucille.

"Yes! And hurry!" said Mo.

Peewee ran away

and got a bedspread.

Aunt Minnie brought Mo a stepladder.

Then Mo put the bedspread

over his shoulder

and climbed to the top of the ladder.

"Good night, birds," he said.

And he threw the bedspread

over the tree.

Suddenly the Bluejays grew quiet.

"Now we wait,"

Mo said in a soft voice.

"Why are they so quiet?"
asked Chicken Lucille.
"They think it's night,"
whispered Mo.
"They've fallen asleep."

26

After fifteen minutes
Mo lifted the bedspread,
and all the Bluejays began to sing.
"Why are they singing?" asked Peewee.

"They think it's tomorrow,"
said Mo.

The fight was over.

"Bravo, Sheriff!" said Aunt Minnie.

"All in a day's work," said Mo.

THE SHADOW

One rainy night Mo sat in his bed
and sipped his tea.

He felt warm and cozy.

"The best part of a sheriff's day
is when it's over," he said.

But suddenly Mo saw the shadow

of a large beast on his wall.

It had hairy wings and a large head.

Mo jumped out of bed.

"Where are you? Come out!" he shouted.

Mo grabbed his tennis racket.
"I'll get you!" he shouted,
and he swung his racket
through the air.

"Are you okay, Sheriff?"
yelled Pearl and Peewee,
banging on Mo's door.
"Go home! Save yourselves!"
Mo shouted.
"I'm after a beast!"
Mo swung his tennis racket
through the air again.

But the shadow of the beast
stayed on the wall.
Mo grabbed a broom.
"Take that!" he yelled,
and he beat the wall
with the broom.

Aunt Minnie and Chicken Lucille
looked in Mo's window.
"Are you all right, Sheriff?"
they yelled.

"Go home! Lock your doors!
I'll get him!" Mo said
and he waved his broom again.

This time Mo hit a moth

that was sitting

near his bedside candle.

"Watch out!" he said to the moth.

"I'm after a beast!"

The moth flew out of the room.

Mo looked back at his wall.

The beast was gone.

"Where did he go?" Mo said.

He looked under his bed,

and he looked in his closet.

"He's gone," Mo said.

"I must have scared him away."

Then Mo stepped outside.

All the animals were gathered
in the rain.

"It's all right now," Mo said.

"The beast is gone.

You can go home."

"Yay! Yay!" The animals clapped.

"Our sheriff has saved us!"

Mo got back in his bed.
"Boy, I'm beat," he said.
"Protecting everyone
can wear you out."

FARAWAY PLACES

One day Mo woke up early.

He washed his face

and brushed his teeth.

Then he sat on his front steps

and looked out at the pond.

"I'm bored," he thought.

"I'm tired of the same pond,
the same faces, the same trees,
the same sky."

Mo went back inside.

He put on a warm jacket
and a wool hat.

Then he packed a suitcase
and walked out
into the cool sunlight.

Mo walked along
the bank of the pond.

"Hi, Sheriff," said Chicken Lucille.

"Where are you going?"

"Faraway places," said Mo.

"And I must go there alone."

"Oh, Sheriff! Don't leave us!"

cried Lucille.

But Mo kept walking.

"Hi, Sheriff," said Pearl and Peewee.

"Where are you going?"

"Faraway places," said Mo.

"Oh, dear!"

cried Pearl and Peewee.

"We'll miss you so much."

"I'll miss you too," said Mo,

"but I must go there alone."

Mo kept walking

and he didn't look back.

He walked into a field

and climbed a big hill.

Near the top of the hill
Mo sat under a tree.
Then he opened his suitcase
and took out a Thermos,
a sweet roll, his glasses,
and a book.

He opened his Thermos

and sipped his tea.

"Good, it's still hot," he said.

He took a bite of sweet roll
and put on his glasses.
Then he picked up his book
and began to read.

"Sheriff," called Aunt Minnie,
"what are you doing?"
"I'm reading a book,"
said Mo.

"What's it about?" asked Peewee.

"Faraway places," said Mo.

"And I must go there alone."

"Oh!" cried Chicken Lucille.

"You're not really leaving us

after all!"

Everyone laughed.

Pearl and Peewee danced a little jig.

Then for the rest of the day

all the animals sat quietly

at the bottom of the hill.

They played cards

as they waited for Mo

to finish his book.

53

Finally it grew dark.

Mo packed up his things

and climbed down the hill.

"Let's go back now,"

he said.

Then Mo and his friends

went over to Aunt Minnie's.

They ate dinner
and talked all night
about faraway places.